Call Me George

CLAIRE SAXBY

Illustrated by Ritva Voutila

sundance™
A Haights Cross Communications Company

The Characters

Georgia

Mom and Dad

Grandad and Grandma

Dan

The Story Setting

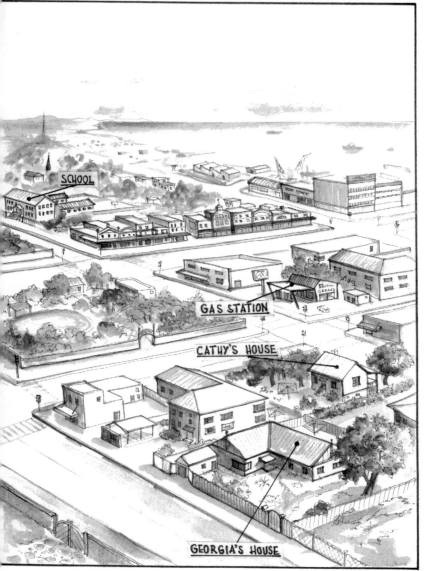

TABLE OF CONTENTS

Call Me George

"I'm changing my name to George!" said Georgia, digging through her clothes.

"But we already have six boys in our family, seven if you include me. You're our only girl," Dad said.

"Where are my jeans?" Georgia stood with her hands on her hips. The contents of her dresser were now on the floor.

"In the wash. They had mud all over them. Why don't you wear your green skirt? Or the pink, floral dress that Grandma bought you?" asked Dad.

"I'm George, and I don't wear skirts or dresses. I wear jeans!" Georgia stomped out to the kitchen.

She sat at the table and watched through the window as the wind blew her jeans around on the clothesline. Why couldn't she have been a boy? Everyone else in the house was a boy except her mom. But she was always at work.

Boys always got to do all the best things. Georgia was green with envy. Boys could ride their bikes to the park by themselves. Georgia always had to go with someone. Boys could wear jeans every day. Georgia had to wear skirts and dresses sometimes.

Georgia looked at the family chores chart. Dan and the others got to mow the lawn. She had to stay inside and help Dad do the cooking. Dan and the others got to help in the yard. She had to help with the laundry. It wasn't fair. Georgia hated the chores chart.

CHAPTER 2

New Blue Jeans

"Here! These were for your birthday."
Dad dropped a new pair of jeans on the
table. "But it seems you need them now."

"Thanks, Dad. You're the best!" Georgia pulled them on as she spoke. "Look, they fit perfectly." The grin on Georgia's face told her dad that they were just right.

Georgia went outside and climbed the crab apple tree. It didn't care if she was a boy or a girl. Up in its leafy branches she was invisible to anyone on the ground.

By the time the gate creaked open and
her brothers got home, Georgia's lap was
full of crab apples, ready to throw.

"Hey! You nearly got me," Pete shouted.

"Good thing it's only Georgia, or we might have been in trouble!" her oldest brother, Tony, said. They laughed.

Georgia lost her temper and threw the crab apples harder. The more she missed, the angrier she got and the worse her aim got.

"There's nothing good about being a girl!" she cried.

Georgia felt the lump in her throat grow, and she blinked away the tears. Her brothers disappeared around the corner. Then she heard the back screen door slam.

Was there anything good about being a girl? Georgia couldn't think of a thing. She felt completely in the dark. She went next door to ask Cathy.

"What's so great about being a girl?" asked Georgia.

"Well, for a start, the clothes are better. We can wear whatever we want. If we want to wear jeans, we can. If we want to wear dresses, we can do that, too."

Cathy pulled a dress from her closet.
She swayed in front of the mirror, her
eyes focused on something far away.
She didn't notice Georgia leaving.

CHAPTER 3

Looking for Answers

Georgia asked Grandad, "Grandad, have you ever wanted to be a girl?"

"Gosh no! If I was a girl, I couldn't have married your grandmother, and we wouldn't have had your mother. Then where would you be?"

Georgia thought he'd missed the point.
He seemed intent on his knitting, so she
didn't ask him any more questions.

Before school the next day, Georgia asked her teacher, "Ms. Ramsay, why can't girls do everything boys can?"

"Why can't they?" Ms. Ramsay turned questions around so that you answered them yourself. "Who says they can't?"

Ms. Ramsay turned back to the board where she was writing math problems. "Why don't you go outside and run around before the bell rings?"

Later, Georgia asked her brother Tony,
"What do you think girls are good at?"

"They're usually better cooks," he said.

He was always hungry. Dad said he could eat a horse and still want dessert.

"But all the best chefs are men." Tony tapped away at the computer. He was designing the costumes for his school play.

Georgia found Grandma fixing a chair. "What's so good about being a girl?"

"Why do you ask, Love?" Grandma used to be a teacher, and like Ms. Ramsay, she answered a question with a question.

"Boys have all the fun. Dad always wants me to do girl things." Georgia didn't mind telling Grandma what was bothering her. Grandma never laughed at her the way her brothers did.

Grandma put the drill down and sat next to Georgia. "What's this really all about?"

"Nothing. Well . . . the school dance is tomorrow, and we have to wear "neat, casual" clothes. I have these new jeans that Dad bought me, but he says I can't wear them to the dance. I have to wear a dress. I hate dresses. You can't do cartwheels. You can't climb trees. You can't do anything in a dress!"

"Do you expect to be doing cartwheels at the dance, then?" Grandma asked.

"No . . . but you know what I mean, don't you, Grandma?" Georgia needed someone to understand.

"Pass me the screwdriver, will you please, Love?" Grandma said.

"Boys can always wear jeans. Why can't girls? It's not fair," Georgia said.

"Girls can . . . usually," said Grandma.

"Why couldn't I have been a boy?" Georgia didn't know whether to cry or throw something. She sat with tears threatening to overflow down her cheeks.

Grandma put down the screwdriver and pulled a tissue out of her pocket. She wiped Georgia's eyes and gave her a hug. Then she looked at Georgia.

"You can do anything you want to. You'll figure it out." She picked up her screwdriver and turned back to the chair.

CHAPTER 4

What to Wear?

Georgia climbed up the crab apple tree to think. Maybe she could wear jeans and pretend she was a boy by putting her hair under a hat. But she always dressed like that, and everyone knew her. If she couldn't wear jeans, then she wouldn't go.

But the dances were always so much fun.
The teachers were in charge, but somehow
they seemed different after school hours.
Some of them even joined in the dancing.

If she wore a dress, everyone would laugh at her. She looked stupid in a dress. But then, all of her friends wore dresses to the dance, even her best friend, Carla.

Maybe it could be a costume dance! She could go as a pirate, wearing jeans. No, then she'd have to shred the legs of her jeans to make the costume look good.

Maybe she could go as a flower child of the 1960s. They always wore jeans. But they decorated their jeans with colored flowers and swirls. There was no way she was painting anything on her new jeans.

Anyway, the dance was tomorrow night, and the school would never change the theme. She'd have to stay home after all.

CHAPTER 5

The Gas Station

The next afternoon, Georgia and her brother Dan rode their bikes to the store. On the way home, they stopped at the gas station to put some air in their tires.

"Shouldn't we ask first?" asked Georgia.

Dan rolled his eyes. "Air is free, Georgia."

Georgia dipped her fingers in the bucket next to the air hose and flicked water at her brother.

"Hey!" Dan dipped his hand in the same bucket and threw a handful of water into Georgia's face. Georgia spluttered, then spied the faucet. She reached down to grab the attached hose.

"Hey! Hey! Stop that!" The owner of the gas station ran toward them, yelling.

Georgia stood up, trying to hide her wet hands behind her back.

"What do you two think you're doing? This is a business, not a playground!"

"We were just . . ." Georgia tried to think of an explanation.

"You were JUST fooling around! JUST get going. Don't let me catch you boys near the water again, or I'll call your parents!" He walked away, muttering to himself.

"What a grump!" Dan said.

But Georgia wasn't listening. "He didn't recognize me. He called me a boy!" Georgia looked down at her red checked shirt and jeans.

All this time she'd wanted to be a boy. Now when someone thought she was, it felt wrong. "He's always been so friendly before . . ." Georgia said.

"Friendly? That guy? Never!"

"The man at the gas station thought I was a boy!" she told Dad when she got home.

"Well, you are wearing your brother's shirt," said Dad mildly, as he stirred the beef stew in the pan.

"Don't you believe me?" Georgia shouted.

"Yes, but why are you upset? I thought you'd give your right arm to be a boy. You should be pleased." Dad opened the oven and took out the apple pie.

"Humph!" said Georgia. She headed to her bedroom feeling down in the dumps.

CHAPTER 6

Big Brother

"So you want to be a boy and do boy things?" Dan flopped down on her bed and bounced a ball against the wall.

"Why?" Georgia was suspicious.

"Well, you could help me mow the lawn tomorrow and dig the garden. Or even better, you could do it by yourself. Then I could help with the cooking like I used to before . . ." He rolled off the bed and caught the ball.

"Before what?" asked Georgia.

Dan sat on the edge of her desk. "Before you got big enough, I helped with the cooking. I HATE mowing the lawn, but it's my turn. If you'd been a boy . . ."

"If I'd been a boy, what?" said Georgia.

"If you'd been a boy, you'd have had to start doing some of the outside chores by now. It's only because you're a girl and the baby of the family that you don't have to. Things are different for you."

"Before you got big enough to help, we all used to swap chores around. Everyone got a turn at everything—laundry, cooking, gardening, chopping wood.

Now you're the only one who doesn't take a turn. You always get to do the cooking." He stood up. "AND you get a room to yourself. NOBODY else does, not even Mom and Dad. It's not fair." Georgia was stunned.

Georgia had no idea that she and Dan were in the same boat. She couldn't believe that Dan was jealous of her. But they agreed on one thing. Why should she be treated differently?

Georgia lay on her bed watching her dreamcatcher spin in the open window. Dan had made it for her last birthday. The feathers quivered gently as the crystals cast colors around her room.

The colored light danced across the walls, making its own patterns. The patterns changed and moved.

"Why can't people make their own patterns?" Georgia whispered. "Why can't I?" she wondered.

Grandma had made her own pattern. Grandad was always inventing his own way to do things. Mom and Dad were making their own patterns, with Mom working and Dad staying home. Maybe she could make her own pattern, too. Georgia smiled. She grabbed a piece of paper, a ruler, and a pen.

"Dan!" she called. "DAAAN!"

CHAPTER  7

A New Pattern

Nobody said anything when Georgia appeared at the dinner table in a dress. Dad was hoping that his only girl might finally be happy to be a girl. But he said nothing.

Grandma was wondering what it was
that had changed Georgia's mind. But
Grandma said nothing.

Grandad looked at Georgia. He knew
something was different, but he couldn't
figure out what.

When dinner was over, Mom drove
Georgia to the dance. Mom didn't notice
the bike shorts Georgia was wearing as
she cartwheeled up the steps.

But Mom did notice the new chores chart on the fridge. The chart gave everyone, even Grandma and Grandad, a turn at every job.

GLOSSARY

chores chart
a list of chores divided
between people

crystals
clear rocks that look
like glass or ice

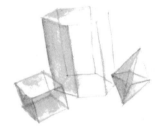

floral
with a pattern of flowers

intent
to be concentrating
on something

muttering
talking under your breath

quivered
shook slightly

recognize
to identify someone
or something

spluttered
talked too quickly,
tripping over the words

Talking with the Author and the Illustrator

Claire Saxby (author)

What did you want to be when you grew up?
A kid.

If there were only two colors in the world, what should they be?
Orange and blue.

Which animal would you most like to be?
A fish.

Ritva Voutila (illustrator)

What's your favorite game?
Chasing my thoughts with pencils and brushes.

Which animal would you most like to be?
One of Santa's reindeers, because I would love to fly around the world once a year.

Published by Sundance Publishing
P.O. Box 1326, 234 Taylor Street, Littleton, MA 01460
800-343-8204
www.sundancepub.com

Copyright © text Claire Saxby
Copyright © illustrations Ritva Voutila

First published 2000 as Sparklers by
Blake Education, Locked Bag 2022, Glebe 2037, Australia
Exclusive United States Distribution: Sundance Publishing

ISBN 0-7608-6974-X

sundance™
A Haights Cross Communications Company